THE FUNNY
FACEOFF

THE FUNNY FACEOFF

Irene Punt

illustrations by
Ken Steacy

Scholastic Canada Ltd.
Toronto New York London Auckland Sydney
Mexico City New Delhi Hong Kong Buenos Aires

Scholastic Canada Ltd.
604 King Street West, Toronto, Ontario M5V 1E1, Canada

Scholastic Inc.
557 Broadway, New York, NY 10012, USA

Scholastic Australia Pty Limited
PO Box 579, Gosford, NSW 2250, Australia

Scholastic New Zealand Limited
Private Bag 94407, Botany, Manukau 2163, New Zealand

Scholastic Children's Books
Euston House, 24 Eversholt Street, London NW1 1DB, UK

Library and Archives Canada Cataloguing in Publication
Punt, Irene, 1955-
The funny faceoff / Irene Punt ; Ken Steacy, illustrator.

ISBN 978-0-545-99681-5

I. Steacy, Ken II. Title.
PS8581.U56F85 2008   jC813'.54   C2007-904460-3

ISBN-10 0-545-99681-3

9 8 7   Printed in Canada 121   13 14 15

Contents

*To Tom — for the day you sang
"Rudolph, the Red-nosed Cowboy"
— I. P.*

Game Time

Snow sat on top of the silver letters that spelled Centennial Arena.

Tom and Stuart lugged their big hockey bags up the stairs and through the entrance doors. They saw one of their buddies and hurried towards him.

"Hey, Mark. Wait up!"

Mark had earphones in his ears and his brother's iPod stuck in his pocket. He turned down the music. "Wait till you guys see what I have in my hockey bag."

They made their way down the hall behind the spectator bleachers to the dressing room, where they propped up their sticks in the corner. The room was crowded.

"C'mon! C'mon!" said Tom. "Let's see!"

Mark reached into his bag. He pulled something out.

"What's that?" Tom asked.

Mark flopped down the sides and sat it upright. He took the iPod out of his pocket and placed it in the slot. "These are mini-speakers. But they make mega sound. Listen to this . . ." He pressed the volume arrow up. "My brother won some free iTunes on The Hockey Flip website."

"Cool!" said Tom.

"We are the champions of the rink . . ." Mark began to sing. He turned up the volume.

"And we make our hockey gear stink
We are the best team
We let off big steam
Toot tooty-toot toot
'Cause we are the champions
of the rink!"

Everyone cracked up. Mark hit the replay button and the song started over. He grabbed his hockey stick and pretended it was a microphone. He sang so loud, his face turned purple.

Everyone stood, cheering and laughing. Everyone . . . except Jordan, the goalie. He was concentrating on lacing his chest pads and tightening the buckles near his ankles. Then he moved into his pre-game stretches.

"I'm trying for a new shutout record," Jordan whispered to Tom. "I gotta focus." He practiced his ugly goalie face.

Tom hoped Jordan got his wish.

The door opened and in walked Coach Howie. He was waving the game sheet and carrying a case of water bottles. Tom liked Coach Howie. He was nice and he was fun. He worked at the Smokin' Cola Company. Sometimes he gave them free energy drinks after a game.

"Okay, you hot dogs," Coach Howie said loudly. A hockey glove flew through the air. Coach Howie blew his whistle. "Settle down. You're Glenlake Hawks, not loony birds. Get your gear on. We've got a game to win!"

Tom pulled on his jersey and began taping his socks, still humming Mark's funny song.

"Which line plays first shift?" asked Stuart.

Coach Howie checked his notes. "I've got Tom at centre; Mark's right wing, Spencer's left wing, and Stuart and Ben are on defence. Jordan's in goal."

Yes! Tom cheered to himself. He looked at his friends. They were all smiling because they all got to play first shift. *We ARE the champions of the rink!* he thought.

Then Stuart caught his finger in the zipper of his hockey bag, Mark pulled on his lucky socks, and Jordan began to hiccup. It was game time.

Go, Hawks, Go!

The team filed out of the dressing room. Tom looked up into the stands. His mom and dad were sitting with Stuart's and Mark's parents. They wore the team colours: yellow and green. Tom's stomach knotted. *Why did he get so nervous before a game anyway?*

The Zamboni swept and flooded the ice, then headed for the parking stall. Coach Howie opened the gate. He took slippery steps across the ice. "Stretch and skate!" he hollered at the Hawks. "Get warmed up." He put the water bottles on the players' home bench. Then he shook hands with the ref.

Tom placed the blade of his stick on the

ice. He took long, slow strides, then picked up speed. Suddenly, his head filled with,

"We are the champions of the rink
And we make our hockey gear stink
We are the best team
We let off big steam . . ."

Mark skated ahead of him, singing the same song.

"Toot tooty-toot toot!" Tom called to him.

Mark bent forward and twisted. *"Toot tooty-toot toot!"*

"Nice stretches," said Coach Howie, cheering them on.

Tom cracked up. The coach had made a joke without knowing it. Tom forgot all about being nervous.

The clock dropped to zero. The buzzer sounded. The Hawks circled around Jordan. "Hawks! Hawks! Hawks!" they cheered. Then the first shift took their starting positions.

Tom set up at centre, his eyes glued to the ice.

The ref dropped the puck and Tom stabbed at it with his stick. The puck flew to Mark. Mark dug in his skate blades and raced up the ice with the puck. He passed it to Tom right before the blue line. Tom wound up and took a slapshot. The Sunridge Sharks' goalie stopped the puck with his blocker, but it rebounded back to Tom. Quickly he fired the puck into the net, hitting the crossbar with a

PING!

"Wow!" cheered Mark and Stuart. They punched Tom on the shoulder. "Great goal!"

The crowd cheered.

The Hawks banged their sticks.

Tom felt great.

"We ARE the champions of the rink!" Mark sang, heading for the bench. Coach Howie held the gate open for them and the next line set up at centre ice.

The song started in Tom's head again and wouldn't quit. Calling themselves champions made him feel more sure and powerful.

"Go, Hawks, go!" cheered the fans.

"Go, Hawks, go!" cheered the players on the bench.

Three periods flew by.

The final score was 4–0 for the Hawks.

Tom headed for the dressing room. He threw his stick in the corner and whipped off his number 15 jersey. He waved it in circles over his head. "Woo hoo!" he shouted.

"Another shutout for Jordan!" announced Mark, both arms in the air. "Another two goals for Tom!" He pressed the power button on the iPod.

*"We are the champions of the rink
And we make our hockey gear stink . . ."*

Everyone sang, swaying in time with the music. Everyone . . . including Jordan.

"Listen up!" shouted Coach Howie. Everyone sat. "Good game, boys. You guys really burned it up out there! For a special treat, I brought you some of the new Rowdy Root Beer we're bottling at the Smokin' Cola Company. Next game is tomorrow at 6:30." He sat down and unlaced his skates as the boys made a beeline for the drinks.

Mark began to sing, making the word "Rowdy" extra loud.

"Ninety-nine Rowdy root beers
on the wall
Ninety-nine Rowdy root beers
If one of those bottles
should happen to fall
There'll be ninety-eight Rowdy
root beers on the wall."

Tom put the open root beer bottle to his lips. Little bubbles fizzled and jumped onto his tongue. He took a big gulp. The fizzles went down his throat and up his nose. He blinked. He pinched his nose. "Did ya feel that fizz?" he asked, eyes watering.

11

"Man, this root beer has gas!" said Mark, rolling his eyes.

The dressing room exploded with laughter.

"You boys are too much!" said Coach Howie, smiling.

"*You're* too much!" the team shouted back. "Thanks for the Rowdy Root Beer, Coach!"

Mark circled the dressing room in his red long underwear, collecting the empty bottles.

Stuart searched for his Band-Aids. And the song went on and on and on . . .

"Eighty-three Rowdy root beers
   on the wall
Eighty-three Rowdy root beers
If one of those bottles
   should happen to fall
There'll be eighty-two Rowdy
   root beers on the wall.

Eighty-two . . ."

Journal Writing

Tom sat at his desk, his journal open. On the way to school he'd thought about what he might write for today. He had lots to say about last night's game. And lots to say about the game tonight. *What should I write first?* he wondered. He glanced at Jordan. Jordan was slowly sharpening his hockey pencil. He looked upset.

"*Psst,*" said Stuart from behind. "Look what I put in my journal." Stuart had stuck an old Band-Aid on the page.

"That's sick," Mark said.

Tom laughed to himself at his friends. They made everything fun. Mark was always cracking jokes. Stuart was smart, but he was accident-prone.

Mrs. Wong, their teacher, walked up and down the aisles, watching them write. She stopped next to Stuart. Tom snickered, wondering what she would say about the Band-Aid.

Mrs. Wong said, "Ouch! Stuart did a journ-*ail* entry. Get it? 'Ail' means sick." Sometimes Mrs. Wong was funny, too. It was like you could say anything to her and it was okay. Then she cleared her throat. "Now, if you're having trouble thinking of something to write, just think about what makes you happy or sad. And don't worry about your spelling. This is *your* journal. It should make you feel good."

Tom put his pencil to the page. For a moment it was stuck. Then he wrote:

I play centre for the Glenlake Hawks.

We had a game last night and we won.

My first goal was a slapshot. My second

goal was a wraparound. AND!!! I almost

got a HAT TRICK — that's three goals!

Can we win tonight? Yes, WE CAN!

We have a new team song.

At the bottom of the page, Tom drew the scoreboard: 4–0. Mrs. Wong *was* right. Tom did feel good, writing about hockey and winning — and scoring goals. He drew fireworks around the score.

Mrs. Wong looked at Jordan. Jordan blushed. When he was in net, wearing his goalie equipment, he looked big and fearless. He could outplay the toughest teams. But when it came to school, he got anxious about some things. Writing and speaking were the worst. His journal was blank today and nothing had been written yesterday either.

Mrs. Wong sighed. "Hmm. If that page stays blank, you'll have to stay in at recess, Jordan."

Tom knew Jordan was embarrassed. He looked around at his other friends. They had a hockey game planned for recess and they needed Jordan.

Mrs. Wong kept circling the classroom. She looked at Amber's work and cooed, "Ooooooh . . . your little white puppy looks sooooo cute."

Jill had already written two pages. "Good work, Jill!" Mrs. Wong said, taking the pencil off her ear. She drew a star on Jill's page.

Kylie's hand waved in the air. "I wrote about my Irish dancing. I went to a *feis* last weekend. That's a dance competition. I wrote about my dress and my music and the big trophy I won."

Mrs. Wong patted Kylie on the shoulder, "It's very nice to be excited about your life, isn't it?" She looked over at Jordan's empty page with a frown. "Better get writing. Remember, a journal entry can be one word or one hundred words. Just be yourself."

Tom thought of something weird while Mrs. Wong spoke. Jordan *was* being himself;

worried and nervous about writing. His blank pages showed that.

Mrs. Wong said, "Maybe you should write about something you're looking forward to."

Tom tried to get Jordan's attention. "Jordan! Jordan!" he whispered, pointing to his Flames jersey. "Write about hockey! That's easy."

Kylie rolled her eyes. "Hockey, hockey, hockey."

Jordan blushed.

Tom blew out a frustrated breath. "Pretend your page is a new sheet of ice that's just been flooded. Carve it up!"

Jordan shrugged. "Okay, okay," he said. "I *am* looking forward to . . ." Carefully he drew the brown root beer bottle from Coach Howie. Then he wrote: **ROWDY**.

Stuart howled when he saw Jordan's page. "That's a journ-*ale* entry! Get it? 'Ale' is beer."

Tom made a face.

Stay Off the Field

The recess bell rang. Tom, Mark, Stuart and Jordan put on their boots and jackets and headed for the caretaker's room.

"Hey, Mr. Mack!" chimed the boys, grabbing the floor hockey sticks from a box.

"Hey, boys!" said Mr. Mack. "How was last night's game?"

"We won!"

Mr. Mack gave them a thumbs-up. "Right on! Now, stay off the field this recess. The entire west side of the school is pure ice."

They headed for the playground. The school cast a black shadow over the field.

"Oh, man," said Stuart, watching his step. "Mr. Mack's right. Yesterday's chinook must've melted the snow into a pond and then it froze solid last night. You could break your leg out there."

"Let's go to the hopscotch area. Nobody ever uses it," suggested Tom. But when they got there, Kylie and her friends had staked it out.

"I'm showing Jill and Amber my Irish dance," said Kylie, both hands on her hips. She kicked up her foot, nearly losing her boot. "I wrote about it in my journal, you know."

"We know," said Mark.

Tom took a tennis ball out of his pocket and dropped it at his feet. He stickhandled it around the girls. Mark clapped sticks with him, stealing the ball.

"Over here!" said Stuart. "Pass it."

"What are you guys doing?" hissed Kylie. "We were here first. And this is where we play *Canadian Idol.* Right now, I'm dancing for my friends. And singing. And you're in our way."

Mark stopped. "Singing? We know a good song!" He winked at Tom, Stuart and Jordan. "Let's sing our face off. Get it? Faceoff!"

"What?" said Jordan.

"Yeah," whispered Mark. "Our special song."

The boys lined up in a row. They held their hockey sticks like microphones.

"One, two, three . . ." counted Mark.

"We are the champions of the rink
And we make our hockey gear stink
We are the best team
We let off big steam . . ."

The boys cracked up. *"Toot tooty-toot toot!"*

The girls giggled. *"Toot toot!"*

Kylie scoffed, "That's an old song from The Flipflops. I know all their songs. I even bought their new CD at the book fair." She cleared her throat and sang, *"Rudolph, the red-nosed pirate . . ."*

Jill stopped Kylie. "Wait! Let's do it together."

"We need their hockey sticks," Amber announced.

Copying the boys, the girls held the sticks and sang,

"Rudolph, the red-nosed pirate,
He had only one good eye,
And if you ever saw him,
You would run away — and die!
Bye-bye!"

They dropped the hockey sticks and waved bye-bye.

Mark clutched his throat and began coughing. "I'm dying, I'm dying. I saw Rudolph, the red-nosed pirate!" he moaned with a raspy voice. "I'm *dying* — to play hockey!" He winked at his friends.

"Woo hoo!" The boys picked up their

sticks and banged them on the cement.

"Wow! I've got an idea!" Kylie shrieked. "Let's ask Mrs. Wong if we can put on a show!"

"I don't want to put on a show," said Jordan. "I hate getting up at the front of the classroom. And I don't do music. I play hockey."

"It wouldn't have to be just music, Kylie," said Amber. "Let's make it . . ."

Tom tried to ignore them. He agreed with Jordan. "Let's just play hockey! This is really annoying. Recess is nearly over!"

Mark reached for the tennis ball. He stick-handled it toward Jordan, then passed it to Tom. Jordan moved into a crouch. Tom fired a shot. Jordan hit the ball, sending it flying toward the field. Stuart ran after it. The instant he set foot on the ice he slipped and fell, scraping his hand raw.

"I need that Band-Aid from my journal," he moaned.

BUZZZZZZ! sounded the bell. The ball rolled to a stop on the ice.

"Everyone inside!" yelled the teacher on recess duty. "Stay off the field."

Tom threw his arms in the air. "Now we don't even have a tennis ball."

—— • ——

Five minutes before the end-of-day bell, Mrs. Wong said, "I've got an idea." She picked up a piece of chalk and wrote on the blackboard:

JOURNAL SHOW AND TELL TOMORROW

"What?" yelped Mark.

"I know, I know. Some of the girls have asked to show off their work. I think it's wonderful to be excited about writing. Keep in mind you can choose whatever you want to tell the class about."

"I'm writing ten more pages about Irish dancing," said Kylie, smiling.

"And I'm bringing props for the show!" said Amber.

"Show?" said Stuart.

"*Show* and Tell!" said Jill. "I'm bringing a tuba."

"Props are not necessary, but they would be nice," said Mrs. Wong. "Just make sure your presentation is only a few minutes."

"Maybe some mothers can make cookies," suggested Amber.

"Yum!" Mrs. Wong smiled. "This *is* going to be fun!"

Tom sunk down in his desk. He liked to get good marks at school and make Mrs. Wong happy. But tonight he didn't have time to do math homework, get extra things like props together and ask his mom to make cookies. He had a hockey game at 6:30!

Tom flipped through his journal. Quickly,

he drew a big unhappy face on the last page.
Inside a speech bubble he wrote,

ARGGHHH!

For some reason, looking at this page
made him feel much better.

Goalie Action

It was 7 o'clock. Westside Arena was freezing. The ref blew his whistle as he raised his arm. "Icing!" The players skated back toward the far faceoff circle, near the Hawks net. As Tom glided across the ice, he glanced at the scoreboard and time clock. It was already second period. The Glenlake Hawks were winning 1–0 against the Westhill Wolves. But

they'd just made a big mistake. And now the Wolves had a chance to score.

Coach Howie stood in the players' box. He had one hand on the gate, one hand on the latch. "Tom! Stuart! Off!" he hollered.

They hustled off the ice; Mark and Spencer launched on.

"Cool it on the hot-dog moves!" said Coach Howie. "No one-man shows out there. We play as a team. Pass the puck. Keep the Wolves guessing. Do your best."

The linesman dropped the puck. The Wolves' number 13 won the faceoff, passing it to his winger. He fired the puck onto the boards. It ricocheted. Their winger knocked the flying puck down with his glove and picked it up on his stick. He took three giant strides and fired the puck at the net. *DONK!* The puck hit Jordan's goalie stick. It rebounded and number 13 was there. *BANG!* He shot the puck again. Jordan's stick

deflected it again. Again number 13 got the rebound. *SHWOOP.* The puck slid and Jordan flew full-stretch, landing on the ice and covering the puck.

The crowd went crazy, screaming and whistling.

The Hawks bench went nuts. "Holy moley, what a goalie!" they yelled, banging their sticks on the boards. Jordan had saved them again.

The linesman grabbed the puck from Jordan and skated to the faceoff circle.

Tom gulped. "Did you see that winger?" he asked Stuart. "And number 13 is bad luck — well, for us."

"Did you see Jordan?" gasped Stuart. "He stopped every shot . . . but can he keep it up?"

Tom and Stuart looked at each other with the same nervous face. "I sure hope so!" they said at the same time.

Thirty minutes later, the Hawks were in the dressing room, dancing.

"We are the champions of the rink
And we make our hockey gear stink
We are the best team
We let off big steam . . ."

"Great game!" cheered Coach Howie. "3–0. ANOTHER shutout for Jordan! But — too many penalties."

Everyone looked at Mark. "Goon!"

"Oops!" he said. And the look on his face said, "Sorry."

Coach Howie opened his hockey bag. Two dozen Rowdy Root Beer bottles sat inside. "Help yourselves!" he said, smiling. "I thought you *smokin'* hot players might need to cool off!"

Everyone laughed. Sometimes Coach Howie was really funny.

Tom, Mark and Stuart opened their bottles.

"*Rowdy!*" said Mark.

They gulped the root beer back.

Jordan put his bottle in his hockey bag, next to the root beer from the day before. "I'm saving mine," he whispered to Tom. "I can never have anything right after a game, until my nerves settle down."

"Hey, I got my prop for tomorrow's journal thing," Stuart announced, pulling off his hockey glove. He showed  everyone his bruised hand with a large Band-Aid on top. The bruise and the Band-Aid were purple, red and green.

"Props!" moaned Mark. "What's with *that*?"

Jordan slouched on the bench, looking miserable. "I don't know what I'm going to do when Mrs. Wong makes me read something from my journal. I always get the hiccups when I'm nervous. And you know what else . . ."

Tom knew. Jordan stuttered if he was super nervous, and he didn't want anyone to notice. Sometimes he stuttered before an important game. But it always went away once he was between the pipes.

Jordan slumped against the wall. The black cage of his helmet dropped down over his face. Suddenly he looked fierce.

Tom had an idea. "I wrote about hockey in my journal. I could bring my Hawks jersey to school for my prop." He shook Jordan's shoulders. "Why don't you wear all your goalie stuff? You could show everyone the mean goalie face you make. And you could show an empty page in your journal and say, 'This is how many pucks got by me this season!'"

Jordan brightened. He thought for a few seconds. "Will I look like a weirdo totally suited up?"

"I'll wear all my equipment, too," said Stuart.

"Me, three," nodded Mark.

"C'mon, Jordan." Tom kept trying. He held his fist out and the boys banged their fists on top.

"Hawks!" they cheered.

Jordan smiled. "You're right. I'm never nervous on the ice, once the game starts. I only get pre-game jitters. Maybe I'll get a shutout at school with my equipment on."

"Make it a *shout*-out!" said Mark. "Get it? Speak up good and *loud!*"

Everyone groaned.

Journal Show and Tell

During lunch hour the next day Tom and Jordan got dressed in the boys' washroom.

"I'm so n-n-nervous," said Jordan. "I'm a l-l-loser."

"You are not. And you'll be great. Just think about our song when you're standing at the front. *We are the champions of the rink!* It'll make you feel strong." Tom smiled. He liked how it felt when he called himself a champion. "C'mon!" He nudged Jordan and together they sang, *"We are the champions of the rink!"*

On the way down the hall, they saw Mr.

Mack in the caretaker's room.

"How's it going?" he asked.

"We are the champions of the rink!" Tom cheered.

"Good going!"

Everyone was scurrying around the classroom, getting ready for the Journal Show and Tell. Amber's mom walked in with a large platter of chocolate cookies. Amber was carrying a shiny gold bag. Out of the top

poked the head of her fluffy white dog, Pickles.

Tom, Stuart and Mark huddled together in a corner of the room, wearing their hockey equipment and jerseys. "Hawks, Hawks, Hawks!" they cheered.

"Hockey, hockey, hockey," said Amber, rolling her eyes.

Jordan's huge goalie pads, gloves and blocker made him look like a giant. He squished himself into his desk, hiccupping so hard his head jolted.

Tom knew Jordan was getting nervous again. "Champion, champion," he mouthed, and winked.

Jordan hiccupped and stuttered, "Th-th-thanks."

Tom looked around the room. *Where's Kylie?* Her desk was empty. *She's the one who wanted to share journals and she's not even here!* Then the weirdest thing happened. Tom heard her voice coming from someone else in the doorway.

"Sorry I'm a bit late, Mrs. Wong. It just takes so long to get my wig on perfectly."

"Oh . . . oh, Kylie!" cried Mrs. Wong, surprised. "I barely recognized you. Your dress is lovely."

Kylie wore a shiny, orange and sapphire-blue dress with tiny, fake diamonds sewn all over it. It had fancy sleeves

and the skirt looked like a huge, open umbrella. Her curly wig was as fluffy and white as Amber's dog, Pickles.

When Pickles saw Kylie he went crazy — barking and growling at her wig. "*Grrrrrrrrrrrrr.*"

"Hush, Pickles." Amber carried him to the back of the classroom so Kylie could sit down.

Mrs. Wong clapped her hands. "People! People! I'm so pleased with this excitement, I could sing. Now, settle down and let's begin."

When everyone was ready, she announced, "I'm going to choose a name." She reached into a box on her desk and pulled out a slip of paper.

"Jill. You go first. Remember, keep it short!"

Jill walked to the front of the classroom, carrying a strange-shaped black case. She unsnapped the clasps and pulled out a large tuba.

From her journal she read:

"My grandpa's tuba was in our basement. My mom said I was too little to play it, but I snuck downstairs and tried anyway. I washed the mouthpiece because Grandpa used to spit when he played it."

Jill sucked in a gulp of air, puffing out her cheeks like a blowfish. She blew out, *"TOOOOOOOT!"* The tuba sounded like a whoopee cushion.

"We could use that tuba for our song," whispered Mark, grinning. *"Toot tooty-toot toot!"*

By two o'clock, more than half the class had shared their journal writing.

Tom looked at his friends. They were all shifting around in their seats, boiling hot. Jordan looked ill. "When's recess?" hissed Mark.

"Soon!" Tom gave him two thumbs up.

Mrs. Wong called out another name. "Kylie."

Kylie's wig and skirt bounced to the front of the classroom. "Yes! It's my turn!" She curtsied and positioned her shiny black shoes. Looking out at her classmates, she began:

Chapter One. Page one of fourteen. I am the best Irish dancer. I have won lots of trophies. I love my costume, my makeup and my wig. I want to get fake eyelashes for my birthday. I want to try out for *Canadian Idol*. I was only four years old when I got my...

"Lovely," said Mrs. Wong. "Unfortunately, we must limit our journal-sharing to one paragraph today."

Kylie frowned as she turned on her music. She began to step and kick and step and kick to an Irish reel. Faster and faster . . . until the end of the tune.

Amber's mother blurted out, "Bravo! Bravo! You students are so gifted. This is a wonderful talent show."

Mrs. Wong read the next name. "Jordan."

Rowdy

Tom, Stuart and Mark all held their breath, watching Jordan pull his goalie bag to the front of the classroom.

"Uh . . ." Jordan froze. He hiccupped. He stuttered, "Uh . . . I-I-I . . ."

Tom waved his arms, trying to get Jordan's attention. "Your helmet!" he coached. "The cage!" He began to hum, *We are the champions of the rink . . .*"

Jordan got his helmet out of the bag, pulled it on and fastened the cage. He let out one last hiccup. Some students snickered. Instantly, Jordan wore his ugly goalie face.

"I am the goalie for the Glenlake Hawks,"

said Jordan in a loud voice. "I love hockey."

Mrs. Wong smiled and nodded.

"My props for today are ..." Jordan looked out at the classroom. Froze for a second. Shook his head. He continued, "My props for today are ... Tom, Mark and Stuart. They're on the Glenlake Hawks, too. I do best when I'm with my team."

A tingle went up Tom's spine. Jordan was FANTASTIC!

The three friends walked to the front of the classroom and stood with their goalie.

"You must read from your journal now, Jordan," said Mrs. Wong. He had never said this much at the front of the classroom. He had never said this much all year. Mrs. Wong looked proud of him.

Jordan opened his journal. He showed the picture he had drawn of the brown root beer bottle. "ROWDY!" he boomed, reading the one word on the page. Then he reached inside his equipment bag and pulled out two Rowdy bottles from the Smokin' Cola Company.

"Huh?" Everyone stood up to see.

Jordan pretended to drink.

"Journal journ-*ale*!" announced Mark.

Stuart said, "*Smokin'*! And full of gas!"

They began to laugh. Then snort. Tom tried to control himself, but he couldn't. Tears were streaming down his cheeks. He held onto his stomach to help with the shooting pains.

"Oh, man," said Mark. "I might laugh my face off. Get it? Faceoff!"

Jordan began to sing, *"Ninety-nine Rowdy . . ."*

Before another word was sung, Amber's mother plunked down the platter of cookies and stormed out of the classroom.

Inappropriate

The boys continued singing,
> *. . . root beers on the wall*
> *Ninety-nine Rowdy root beers*
> *If one of those bottles*
> *should happen to fall*
> *There'll be ninety-eight Rowdy*
> *root beers on the wall."*

Mrs. Wong cleared her throat. "Ahem. That song is from an old camp song. Now for the next student to share . . ." She put her hand into the box filled with names.

Knock, knock. Dr. Dean, the school principal, was standing in the doorway. "I'd like to see these boys now, please — Jordan, Mark, Stuart and Tom. Thank you."

——— • ———

The boys sat down in a row on the chairs inside Dr. Dean's office. Tom's face felt hot. His heart was beating fast. He'd never been inside the principal's office before and she was not smiling.

"Can you boys guess why I've called you into my office this afternoon?" Dr. Dean was serious.

The boys looked at each other, puzzled.

"Come on," said Dr. Dean. "Think about your actions."

"Is it for going on the frozen field?" asked Stuart, showing his bruised hand and scab.

"No." Dr. Dean wrote notes. "But that is another reason to speak with you. The field is closed — and you are to keep off."

"Were we late after lunch?" asked Tom, remembering how they had said hello to Mr. Mack.

Dr. Dean wrote another note. Then she said, "I've just received a parent complaint about your choice of songs and props for a class presentation. We don't have inappropriate songs sung at our school. Perhaps you learned this one in your hockey dressing room. And singing it at school could be cause for suspension."

Tom felt like he'd been hit in the stomach with a puck. "Does suspension mean what it means in hockey?" he asked Dr. Dean. "In hockey, you miss the next game."

Dr. Dean nodded. "In school you miss the next DAY."

Tom glanced at his friends. They all looked confused and sick.

"I didn't know we couldn't sing that," squeaked Mark. "I've heard something like it sung on the school bus."

Dr. Dean wrote more notes.

"Does 'inappropriate' mean doing the wrong thing at the wrong time?" asked Stuart. "I was going to show everyone my Band-Aids — with no blood or anything. Is that inappropriate?"

Tom took a deep breath. *What would his parents say?* To hold back his tears, he told himself over and over, *Champions. We are the champions*. But he didn't feel like one at all.

Jordan cleared his throat. "Um . . . um . . . We're here be-be-because I read my j-j-journal," he stuttered. "And . . . be-be-because . . ." He hiccupped and his face went bright red.

Dr. Dean tapped her pencil.

Then Jordan dropped the cage down on his mask and said firmly, "We were told we could bring props for when we shared our journal. I wrote about Rowdy root beer, so I showed everyone the bottles I had. It's a new drink. Then we sang 'Ninety-Nine Rowdy Root Beers on the Wall.' We only started laughing because we were nervous." He paused. "Everyone thinks hockey players don't get nervous, but I do."

"Me, too," said Tom. "I get nervous."

"Oh," said Dr. Dean. Her lips twitched. Her forehead scrunched. "Ninety-nine bottles of *root* beer! That's a bit different from the message I got. Jordan, you've done a good job of explaining your side of the story. You speak very well."

Jordan smiled as he lifted the cage of his goalie helmet.

Tom began to wonder. How did Dr. Dean get everything so mixed up? What did she *think* they sang?

KNOCK, KNOCK, KNOCK!

Three loud raps on Dr. Dean's door interrupted them. "Dr. Dean," said Mr. Mack. "We have a problem on the field."

"What is it?" Dr. Dean asked.

"Amber took Pickles outside for recess, and the dog ran right to the middle of the field," explained Mr. Mack. "He saw a tennis ball."

Dr. Dean stared. Tom gulped. It was his tennis ball.

Mr. Mack continued, "Pickles won't move and nobody can walk on the ice. What should we do?"

"Oh, dear," said Dr. Dean. "Dogs are not allowed on the field. Ever. It's a city bylaw!" She sharpened her pencil.

The Funny Faceoff

"Pickles! Picky!" screamed Amber. "Come here, Picky!"

Mrs. Wong, Amber's mother and the students were lined up at the edge of the field, all eyes on the little dog. Tom, Stuart, Mark and Jordan hurried toward them, with Mr. Mack and Dr. Dean not far behind.

"*Arr-ooo. Arr-ooo*," whined Pickles weakly.

"He's scared. And he might freeze," sobbed Amber. "I have to rescue him." She took one step onto the ice. *Swoosh!* She wiped out.

Mr. Mack slid to Amber's side and lifted her up by the elbow. *Boom!* They both fell.

"*Ouch!*" yelped Mr. Mack, rubbing his elbow. "Close call. I could have cracked my head open on this ice. *Nobody* can walk on this field until the ice melts."

"It might not melt for a *week!*" exclaimed Amber. "Pickles will *starve*."

The class stared out across the field. Mrs. Wong tightened her scarf and pulled down her hat. She blew into her mitts. "Hmm. This is a problem."

"A big problem," agreed Dr. Dean.

Jordan said, "I'm not afraid of thick, hard ice." He knocked on his goalie helmet.

"Me, neither," said Tom. "Our hockey

equipment is made for it." He studied Pickles. Pickles had the tennis ball in his mouth. Tom had an idea. "We just need our sticks!"

"I'll be right back," said Mr. Mack, catching on. While Mrs. Wong's class shivered at the edge of the field, he hurried to get their sticks from the classroom. By the time he returned, Tom, Jordan, Stuart and Mark had tightened their boots and helmets. They took their sticks and looked at Dr. Dean.

"Well . . . I guess we can allow you hockey players to go onto the ice," she said.

"Be careful!" warned Mrs. Wong, as Stuart and Mark headed toward the stranded dog.

"Please save Pickles," begged Amber. *"Pleeeease!"*

"Here, Pickles," called Stuart. "Come here, Pickles."

· Pickles cocked his head, then danced for

the boys in the middle of the field. Stuart and Mark moved in quickly. Like wingers, they spread out around the dog. Suddenly, Pickles started to run toward busy Elbow Drive.

"The cars! The cars!" shouted Mark, running and sliding as fast as he could. "Pickles has a breakaway with the ball!" Mark fell face down. He picked himself up.

"Pickles!" snapped Stuart. "Sit! You sit!" Stuart fell backward.

Pickles stopped and turned. He wagged his tail. The look in his eyes said, "*Na na na na.* You can't catch me!"

"Stuart! Mark! Go the other direction!" Tom hollered. "Circle back toward the school. Pickles thinks we're playing a game with him. We have to outfox him."

Stuart and Mark turned, following Tom's suggestion. Pickles chased after them — away from Elbow Drive.

"Go, Hawks, go!" shouted the students.

There was more to do — and fast. Tom looked at Kylie. "Can I borrow your wig?" Kylie made a face, but then she took it off and handed it to Tom.

Then he and Jordan headed out on the ice.

Tom called, "Pickles! Picky, Picky, Pickles!" He shook the curly, white wig. "Come here, Pickles. I have a little dog for you to meet." Tom barked like a yappy dog.

Pickles looked at him and at the wig. Tom barked again and then dropped the wig on the ice. He stepped back. "Set up for a face-off!" he shouted to Stuart and Mark.

Tom kept his stick on the ice, ready for Pickles. The dog pranced toward the wig, the tennis ball still in his mouth. Then he dropped the ball to sniff the wig. Tom's plan had worked! Quickly he grabbed the tennis ball with his stick and passed it to Stuart.

"*Arf! Arf!*" barked Pickles, charging after the ball.

"Go, Hawks, go!" shouted the students standing on the edge of the field, watching Pickles go against the Hawks.

Stuart took a shot, firing the ball toward Jordan. Pickles bolted after the flying ball. It landed. It bounced. Jordan kept a solid goalie stance as Pickles slid across the ice. Then Jordan flew full-stretch, landing on the ice — and covering Pickles.

The students went crazy, screaming and

whistling. "Yaay!" they yelled. Jordan had the dog.

"*Aarrrrr-ooooo,*" Pickles howled.

Tom, Stuart and Mark circled around Jordan and his captive. As they walked carefully off the icy field, they sang,

"We are the champions of the rink
And we make our hockey gear stink
We are the best team
We let off big steam . . ."

Jordan handed Pickles to Amber. Amber gushed, "Thank you, thank you, *thank you!*"

Tom felt proud. He looked at everyone's happy face. Then he noticed Dr. Dean shaking her head. Tom gulped. *Is Dr. Dean shaking her head in a good way or a bad way?* It was hard to tell.

"Do you think we're in the doghouse?" asked Mark.

Finally, Dr. Dean spoke. "Well done."

Champions of
the Rink

Back in the classroom, Mrs. Wong held the box of names for Journal Show and Tell. She pulled out a name. "Tom. It's your turn."

Tom walked to the front of the classroom, carrying his journal. He opened it and began looking for something to read. "Nope. Nope," he mumbled. Every journal entry he had made was about hockey. And now he wasn't sure what was good to read in school, and what wasn't.

"Please, Tom," said Mrs. Wong. "I'd like to hear from everyone this afternoon, if possible."

Tom looked up. "Can Mark, Stuart and Jordan be *my* props?" He winced.

"Oh, boy," said Mrs. Wong. She took a deep breath. "Okay."

Mark, Stuart and Jordan filed up and stood beside Tom. He pointed to the journal entry he'd done about their funny hockey song. "Let's sing this one," he whispered.

"Are you *crazy?*" asked Stuart.

"But I have a good idea." Tom looked at Mrs. Wong. "We need a thirty-second time out for a team meeting!"

Mrs. Wong nodded.

Tom whispered something to his friends. Then they stood in a line. They positioned their wet feet. They bowed, and began to sing:

"We are the champions of the rink
And we make our hockey gear . . ."

They paused. The girls shouted out, "Stink!" And Jill got ready to toot her tuba.

Mrs. Wong raised her eyebrows. She shook her head at the girls.

The boys started over.

"We are the champions of the rink
And we make our hockey gear . . .
   THINK!
We are the champions
We work together
Good friends forever
'Cause we are the champions
   of the rink!"

They bowed again. "THE END!" they

shouted, pumping their fists in the air.

"What?" said Kylie. "That's not right. The song doesn't go like that. You missed the best part — with the toots."

Kylie got one of Mrs. Wong's looks as the boys returned to their desks.

Mrs. Wong clapped enthusiastically. "Today, you Hawks were champions on ice, rescuing Pickles. It was just like a hockey rink out there!"

"Yay, Hawks!" everyone cheered.

Four Hawks smiled from their seats.

Today was weird, Tom thought. *First, we did the wrong thing at the wrong time — according to Amber's mom. Then Dr. Dean got the wrong thing wrong. Then we did the wrong thing at the right time — by going onto the ice to rescue Pickles. Only Jordan had done the right thing at the right time. He had done a great job of explaining to the principal.*

Tom looked around at his friends. *It's nice to be a team. Together, maybe we can figure out how to do the right thing at the right time — every time.*

Hockey rules! Tom thought. He couldn't wait for the next game.